Isaac Bassett Choate

With Birds and Flowers

Isaac Bassett Choate

With Birds and Flowers

ISBN/EAN: 9783337105549

Printed in Europe, USA, Canada, Australia, Japan

Cover: Foto ©Andreas Hilbeck / pixelio.de

More available books at **www.hansebooks.com**

WITH BIRDS
AND FLOWERS

BY

ISAAC BASSETT CHOATE

" One side small birds singing,
On the other, fresh flowers springing."
—Old Song.

NEW YORK
HOME JOURNAL PRINT
1895

Contents.

Contents.

Contents.

Contents.

PINE GROSBEAK.

Beneath the lowering skies
    Low-hanging, cold and gray,
The frozen runnel lies
    A voiceless stream to-day;
Its life went with the summer bird,
In nature now no song is heard,
    No strains of music rise
        From spirits light and gay.

The falling flakes of snow,
    On downy pinions white
Light dancing to and fro,
    Affect a mimic flight;
They gather as the birds in flocks
Low hover over sands and rocks
    Uncertain where to go,
        Uncertain where to light.

To bramble by the wall,
    Dry grass and golden-rod,
Sweet fern and thistlo tall,
    Milkweeds of silky pod,
There comes another flock so gay
Of grosbeaks from the north to-day;
    With merry note they call,
        Greet us with wink and nod.

Warm-hearted northern bird,
    A new-year's wish you bring,
No other song is heard,
    Is seen no other wing;
How warm the colors of your dress!
This gloomy day our eyes they bless;
    Had I the fitting word,
        Your praises would I sing.

ALDER BLOOM.

Still pussy-willow folds her hands
  Close wrapped in muff of snowy fur,
Knee-deep in snow impatient stands
  Awaiting earliest bee astir.
There seems no other bush awake
  Along the margin of the stream,
No stir of sap is felt to break
  The magic of the winter's dream.

Now lady birch from melting snow
  Lifts trailing robe with dainty hand ;
Lithe alder bushes, bending low,
  In reverence about her stand.
While birch and willow hesitate
  To choose a color to their taste,
These ardent beaux, without debate,
  Their tasseled gold put on in haste.

11

SNOW BUNTINGS.

Brave hearts ! bold spirits stoutly venturing forth
From the inclement North !
Your slender, graceful forms
Braving the winter's cold, the winter's icy storms !

Late coming with the biting winds that blow,
That drive the falling snow,
Whirling it everywhere,
With giddy dancing flakes filling the darkened air,

You bring into the gloom of these short days
Bright thoughts of sunny rays
To light our landscape soon,
To kindle to a burning heat our summer's noon.

Nurslings of snow and ice, on frozen ground
Your lone home nest is found,
Beside the Polar Sea
Where groans and moans the ice in agony.

Perchance in all your life you have not seen
The fields and forests green ;
Seen maple buds unfold
And dandelions weave rare cloth of gold.

You have not heard, perchance, the running streams,
Nor in your happiest dreams
The liquid music heard
With which on summer eve wooes kindred bird.

What charms can we not offer for delay,
If you will only stay
Till the blithe swallow comes,—
Till round the orchard trees the honey-storer hums!

Then shall you watch, delighted at the sight,
The swallow's darting flight;
With wonder then shall see
Bright rainbow-colored butterfly and bee.

Then shall there flash before your dazzled eyes
The wealth of tropic dyes
On ruby-throat;—but no,
You would be homesick for the pure white snow!

PUSSY-WILLOW.

A dream of blossoms in the orchard trees,
 Of flowers bright in garden and in field,
Of sweets distilled within the cups of these,
 Of stores of honeyed nectar they will yield;

A dream of sunshine filling earth and skies,
 Of sweetest fragrance borne on summer breeze,
Of birds familiar and of butterflies,
 Haunts in their cells the winter-sleeping bees.

A dream of bluebirds coming back in spring,—
 Some flecks of color fallen from the sky,—
Of merry songs the wrens and linnets sing,
 Of cricket's chirp and swallow's twittering cry;

A dream of waters singing as they go,
 Where over bending grass they softly slip,
Of her own beauty seen in pools below,
 Thrills Pussy-Willow to each downy tip.

For dreams like these the willow cannot sleep,
 Nor bee rest easy in his cloister cell;
Both wake at once from slumber long and deep:—
 One common thought gives common life as well.

KINGLET.

With best of rights has Nature crowned you king,
For while we say, "Poor little chilly thing,
Waiting as we for spring!"
You then begin to sing,
And all the pine woods with the music ring.

How with delight our weary souls are stirred
To see your royal person ruffed and furred!
Your sweet song plainly heard
Comes as prophetic word
To tell of summer flower, of summer bird.

Beneath the sheltering pine, the hemlock tree,
All winter long your busy life we see,
Mark well how you agree
With comrades two or three;
Blithe neighbor, you, of wren and chickadee.

With joy through falling flakes do we behold
Your flaming crown of orange set in gold,
Worn with an air as bold
As, in midwinter cold,
Wears titmouse jaunty cap in field and wold.

Midsummer with its ardor does not please,
With you the rigor of the North agrees;
But when our rivers freeze
You quit the Arctic seas,—
Come here to stay with us, with chickadees.

SAXIFRAGE.

Pale nurslings of the early waking year,
  Forerunners of the coming spring,
    Shy creeping round the edge
    Of broken granite ledge
Soon as the drifts of winter disappear;
  Your tender rootlets fondly cling
    Close in the frost-made rifts,
    Your slender stalk uplifts
Sweet clustering flowers of hope our waiting hearts to
    cheer.

You claim no favored spot of meadow ground
  Where violets and daisies grow,
    But o'er earth's bosom bare
    You softly venture where
No other seemly covering would be found;
  You brave the wintry winds that blow
    Through withered grasses sere,
    Wait patiently to hear
Young bright-eyed, golden buttercups glad waken all
    around.

BLUEBIRD.

The summer sunshine filtering through
  The birch trees leaning o'er the stream,
Falls flashing bright on waters blue,
  In flecks that to my fancy seem
White lilies bathed in morning dew,—
    Sweet image true,
    Dear Love, of you,—
As on the river's breast they dream.

Upon the mossy bank I lie
  And, looking upward through the trees,
See fleecy clouds go drifting high
  Upon the æther's azure seas,
Calm sailing on before my eye,
    Till cloud and sky
    Are rippled by
The light leaves veering in the breeze.

This minds me of that wintry day,—
  The winds of March were blustering,
The snow-flakes, joined in frolic gay,
  Whirled round in many a magic ring;
A rift of blue shot through their play,—
    More mad than they,
    I hailed that day
The bluebird, harbinger of spring.

HEPATICAS.

Shyest of Nature's brood,
Retreating to the wood,
Just at its edge a refuge have ye found;
Like partridge chicks in fright,
Keeping yourselves from sight
Under the dry leaves scattered on the ground;

Ye would not shrink so much
From our fond sight and touch
If only our hearts' feeling could be known;
We wait with watching eyes
To mark your mild surprise
That, coming early, ye come not alone.

The bluebird yesterday
Came flying home this way,
He piped his very sweetest song of you;
In fullest faith and love
We are now come to prove
That bluebird's prophecy shall turn out true.

We push the leaves away,
And there in silken gray
Has Nature swaddled tenderly your forms;
Open for us your eyes!
Look to the April skies
Blue as in summer after heavy storms!

Within the opening lid
A thought of blue is hid,
A memory of skies watched long ago;
A dream ye fondly kept
All that long night ye slept
Beneath the downy coverlets of snow.

PINE LINNET.

High up among the dark green boughs of pine
    That lift and sway in breath of passing breeze,
    Hang sweet-toned harps æolian, 'mong the trees
They voice a spirit's mood akin to mine;

A mood of sober reverie and thought
    Close bordering on the mystery of dreams
    In which the memory of childhood seems
A picture from the Land Eternal brought.

Low chiming with tnat wind-played melody,
    A soft, sweet, sympathetic song is heard,
    The tender outburst of a tuneful bird
Whose slender note swells Nature's harmony.

Shy linnet in the pine tops high above,
    We watch thee flitting oft from bough to bough,
    We listen to thy cheerful singing now,
A heartfelt note in Nature's song of love.

Was it the summer wind's bewitching voice
    That called thee to the pine woods lone to-day
    As it so often calls myself this way
To hear a world of innocence rejoice?

ANEMONES.

Fair children of the youthful spring,
Whose forms so slender rock and swing
  In March winds roughly blowing;
Our summer friends are on the wing,
Already merry bluebirds sing,
  The brookside flag is growing.

Ye brave the cold and squally skies
In bleak and open fields where flies
  The cloud's unresting shadow;
Where wasting drift by stone wall lies,
And slow the oozing water dries
  From brown grass-matted meadow.

Where strongest blows the chilly blast
On eastern slopes your lot is cast,
  There do ye wait contented;
By wood hepaticas are massed;
In sunny corners sheltered fast
  Are dandelions tented.

As videttes are ye posted out
The guard advanced of summer's scout,
  Her corps of observation;
Your snow-white petals boldly flout
Ensigns of Winter in a rout;
  He yields his domination.

REDWING BLACKBIRDS.

On tiptoe leafless birch and willow stand
In alder swamp half water and half land,
Their slender twigs just showing faintest green,
　While down among the dead and broken flags,
　Impatient of the spring that idly lags,
Thick sprouting shoots are seen
　Pushing the leaves aside ;
As, waking on the sunny slopes of ground,
Anemones and liverworts are found
　With violets blue-eyed.

Now comes a flock of redwings chattering wild,
As happy in their coming as the child
That welcomes to the North the summer bird,
　When all the winter long in field and grove
　No gaily painted wing was seen to move,　-
No gushing song was heard
　Filling the world with glee,
As now do blackbirds from the ash tree tall
Ten thousand times repeat their noisy call,
　"Chur-ree, chur-ree, chur-ree!"

MAYFLOWERS.

Sleeping, soundly sleeping in Nature's close em-
    bracing,
  Quiet lie the daisies beneath the downy snow;
Leaping, gaily leaping, in maddest frolic racing,
  Squirrels weave the mazes of footprints to and
    fro.

Creeping, softly creeping, oh, so shy and fearful!
  Grope the mayflowers blindly beneath the fallen
    leaves;
Weeping, sorely weeping, oh, so sad and tear-
    ful!
  Bending low and kindly the sky of April grieves.

Keeping, closely keeping as a jealous lover,
  Nature's breast affrighted conceals her precious
    prize;
Peeping, coyly peeping through the wet leaves'
    cover,
To a world delighted Mayflower opes her eyes.

BROWN TITLARK.

Soon as the measured stroke we hear
  Of northward flying fowl in spring,
Dear little titlark's piping clear
Chimes in with notes of hearty cheer
  Which merry bluebirds sing.

We know not if from east or west,
  From south or north, he took his flight;
Titlark is here as much at rest
As if this spot he loved the best,
  He is contented quite.

As busy as the prudent bee,
  Of spirits ever light and gay,
He so much flatters us that we
Are in the hope confirmed that he
  All summer long will stay.

But when brisk robin's call we hear,
  When blackbirds chatter later on,
In gladdest season of the year,
While day by day new friends appear,
  Behold, titlark is gone!

DANDELIONS.

Dear gipsy flowers that love so well
To neighbor with the pimpernel,
By trodden paths of men to dwell
    In humble guise,
Your lives and fortunes plainly tell
    That ye are wise.

Soon as the snowdrifts disappear,
We find you thickly flocking here
As bluebirds come with notes of cheer,
    With songs of May;
Until the waning of the year
    With us ye stay.

Grouped on the greensward here and there
Your tents are pitched with little care
Only to shun the chilly air
    From north lands blown,
Your courts kept open to the fair
    Round sun at noon.

Fearless of morning's robber bold
Who steals the pearls your petals hold,
Your wealth of nightly hoarded gold
    Ye wide display,
And all your treasure rich unfold
    To light of day.

Gay buttercups and golden-rod,
Of gentle mien, with gracious nod
Greet you uplooking from the sod,
    But fixed your gaze
Upon the sun's round face and broad
    Through summer days.

On Earth's green mantle set as bright
As spangles on the robe of Night,
Daily up-springing to our sight,
    To you 'tis given
In myriad groups to rival quite
    The stars of heaven.

ROBIN.

Adown the field the ploughman whistling goes,
 One foot upon the sod one in the furrow,
The robin hops along, companion close,
 In search of worm turned out of winter burrow;
One thinking of the bairns he loves the best
 At home within the tender care of mother,
Poor little fledglings chirping in the nest
 Unceasing anxious cares give to the other.

Both happy as the bright hours of the day,
 Rejoicing each in other as a neighbor,
Both conscious of the love that doth repay
 The careful, wearying toil of daily labor;
The burden of both hearts is borne by song
 Light on the summer breeze, in music swelling,
Sweet notes that simple melody prolong,
 Of home and homely joys how plainly telling!

VIOLETS.

Sweet nestlings in the hearts of living men
Who love you for yourselves, and yet again,
Because their mothers loved you in their youth
When, toiling in the meadows as toiled Ruth
Among the reapers of the golden corn,
They loved your bloom as, later, their first-born.

Spring's darlings are ye, yet all summer through,
Through all the winter time is Nature true
To tender thoughts of violets in the grass,
Not from her memory does your sweetness pass;
When Spring returns, the blue of April skies
Just matches blue we see in your soft eyes.

When in your beds ye wake from slumber sound,
See dandelions waking all around!
See how on bending stems their green cups hold
Their old-time store of bright, untarnished gold!
See, in this April sky, last April's blue!
Believe as little changed men's love for you!

CUCKOO.

What do I hear?
Is it from far or near?
Is it upon the left or right,
From down below or from the height,
The sound of any living, vocal thing?
Or is it only the vain conjuring
Of artist Fancy shaping large and clear
What dryads hear?

It seems the beat
Of silence - sandalled feet
As Echo flies from hill to hill,
Across the vale, across the rill;
She bears that note as soft as is the flight
Of owl low shadowing a mouse at night,
That sound mysterious she doth repeat
From lone retreat.

I wonder who
Would think that low "Cuckoo!"
From April's budding thickets heard,
Was call of any waiting bird
That had outstripped its fellows on the wing
In eager haste to herald coming Spring?
    Its faint voice calling, soft and low,
    "Cuckoo! Cuckoo!"

Who only knew
The calling of cuckoo
Might think he listened to the ghost
Of some voice in these shadows lost:
The loneliness embodied in that tone
Seems by itself to wander all alone
    The deep recesses of the woodlands through,
    Calling, "Cuckoo!"

SPEEDWELL.

Fair flowers, modest, shy,
  In depths of billowy meadow grasses hiding,
And yet worn footpaths nigh
  Is found the wonted place of your abiding
To watch with curious gaze the passer-by!

Your eyes, wide open, tell
In tone of Saxon blue your heart's warm feeling:
  As from the hermit's cell
Shines midnight lamp his piety revealing,
  The fragrant breath of flowers bids me, "Speed well!"

How gladly fain would I
  This long bright summer's day in dreaming squander,
Among the flowers lie,
  My footsteps ceasing for a space to wander,
But cares of love force me to say, "Good-bye!"

WELCOMING THE SWALLOW.

Across the land, across the spacious sea,
  One course unchanging kept all that long way,
  More than a thousand miles since yesterday
Have you from tropic climes come back to me.

Not pausing in that flight until you saw
  The broad-roofed barn with ample sheds around,
  Beneath their eaves and on their rafters found
Long rows of swallow-nests of mud and straw.

Close are these ranged in friendly neighborhood
  As village streets where kindred tribesmen dwell,
  Of equal fortune all — you know them well —
Know cautious parents and adventurous brood.

Now are you back again with twittering song,
  With flight impatient darting to and fro,
  Awaiting summer friends of long ago
As for your coming we have waited long.

Now may you fancy our great loneliness
  While snowy fields no swallow's singing knew;
  With what deep longing all the winter through
We've waited for your coming, you may guess.

INNOCENTS.

Is it a gossamer veil rich woven in threads of light,
    Filmy fabric of mist from the vapor over the stream,
Or have the mischievous fays unraveled the moonbeams
      at night,
    Weaving the lines anew to the tissue fine of a dream ?

Where lay the pasture and field not more than a fortnight
      ago
    Sleeping their winter sleep as sound as do swallows at
      night,
Only the hardhack and fern broke through the blanket
    of snow,
    In the turns of the zigzag fence dry mulleins and
    thistles in sight ;

Then from the splintered stub the caw of the crow was
    heard,
    Perchance in the lilac bush the back of a bluebird was
    seen ;
To-day is the world alive to the boy, the bee, and the
    bird,
    Now the buds on the lilac sprouts are bursting with
    purple and green.

Dame Nature is waking below, where the roots of the
    grasses creep,
Where, crushed to a spiral whorl, the leaves of the
    mullein lie,
Keeping, in thought or in dream, the form of the rose
    while they sleep,
Loose scattered over the sod as stars are set in the
    sky.

Here doth she wake with a smile beneath that magical
    veil
Which is drawn by an unseen hand to replace the van-
    ishing snow ;
Tinged with the faintest of blue is that delicate covering
    pale   .
Over her worn face spread where the blossoming inno-
    cents grow.

CHIPPING SPARROW.

Not for the gift of song,
  Low, liquid flutings from the thrush's throat,
Poured steadily and long,
Poured tenderly yet strong
  In one melodious air of varied note,
Do we the coming greet
  Of our old neighbor in the early spring;
Enough that she repeat
That one note soft and sweet
  Which all her kindred have been taught to sing.

Not for a proud array
  To match the splendor of the oriole's coat,
Not for the colors gay,
Bright rainbow tints that play
  Over the plumage of the ruby-throat,
This April day do we
  Hail you, old neighbor, after months of snow;
Enough that you agree
With us that our roof-tree
  Is just the pleasantest of all that grow.

ANDROMEDA.

All winter long beneath the level snow,
  Crushed down and frozen in its watery bed
The pliant shrub, Andromeda, below
  Has slept as soundly as if she were dead:
Now that these April winds begin to blow,
These freshet-swollen runnels noisy flow,
  The waking plant lifts gracefully her head,
  Her slender twigs outspread.

All ready for the soft south winds to swing
  Hang ivory bells the drooping spray along
To chime in with the thrushes when they sing
  And swell the choral chant of Nature's song,
What matters it we cannot hear them ring?
To Fancy's ear their swaying movements bring
  A rich melodious rhythm sweet and strong
  Spring's praises to prolong.

Reminding of Andromeda the peer
  Of Juno held, divinest of the fair,
Who challenged Nereus' daughters without fear
  Her charms would suffer any by compare;
For this presumption she was fastened near
The water's edge, left without pitying tear
  To meet a cruel fate, till rescued there
  By Perseus bold to dare.

WOODPECKER.

A quick, sharp cry of anguish or of fright,
  A piercing note and clear,
A gray bird winging labored, drooping flight,
  Woodpecker now is here.

We watch him climb the hemlock, slow and sly,
  The rough bark closely scan
Peer round the tree-trunk furtively and shy
  As if afraid of man.

How has he learned our presence so to dread,
  To shrink from human sight?
Is it instinctive, in his nature bred,
  Companionship to slight?   .

Is it survival from that ancient day
  When — daughter of the sun —
Fair Circe met a huntsman in the way —
  Her love that moment won?

Venilia's spouse unmatched by mortal foes,
  Unhurt by mortal arms,
Had not protecting buckler to oppose
  Against the sorcerer's charms.

Beneath her potent wand's transforming power
  Was hunter changed to prey;
Tradition says that from that luckless hour
  Venilia pined away.

'Tis for woodpeckers well, perhaps, that they
  From human glances hide,
For these can weave as strong a spell to-day
  As any Circe tried.

HEARTSEASE.

Playmate and cousin of maid Violet,
  Through meadows strolling with her, hand in
    hand,
You look up from the grasses dewy wet
Through tears upon your lashes shining yet
  Before the sun has dried or breezes fanned,
Or early milkmaid with her swain has met;
Towards the brightening east your face is set
  As Parsee worshipper in Persian land,
Or strictest devotee of Mahomet.

Heartsease we call you for the blessed sight
  Of sweet contentment with your humble lot,
Enough for you to share the dew of night
With Violet, and with her greet the light,
  Or bear the chilly winds, complaining not.
Your patient love is seen, if read aright
Tho mild expression of your features bright
  Serenely overspread with earnest thought,
Which coming to our hearts wins entrance quite.

WARBLER AND TITMOUSE.

Yellow warbler creeping
Softly, shyly peeping
Through the trembling needles of the whispering pine,
Thou dost watch unsleeping,
On my movements keeping
Just as sharp a lookout as I would keep on thine.

Busy at your labor,
Calling to your neighbor,
Little black-cap titmouse, with your cheery "tweet!"
Life goes on how gaily,
Sharing duties daily
With your fellow-worker in companionship so sweet!

You a recent comer
And only for the summer
From the jaunty black-cap receive a welcome warm;
You should tarry longer,
Till the cold is stronger,
To hear his merry piping in the bleak December storm.

Dream not, pray, of danger
From the curious stranger
Standing by the tree-trunk and closely watching you
Charming bit of yellow,
More charming yet your fellow
Who will stay to cheer with music the long cold win-
ter through.

AQUILEGIA.

Bright bits of color—red and orange blending—
  Hung out from clefts of ledges bleak and bare,
On slender branches of a plant low bending,
  Slow swinging idly on the summer air,
      So tender and so frail,
      Bold challenging the gale;
      High ledges suiting best
      Where eagles build their nest!
From those wild freedom-loving neighbors came
Fair Aquilegia's name.

Your stately kin-flower, on rich meadows growing,
  Courts not the north wind's rude and rough caress,
Nods to the warm, sweet breeze of summer going
  On sandalled feet that grass blades softly press.
      Light poised on easy wing
      Its purple blossoms swing
      As doves just taking flight,
      Or hovering to alight.
From timid doves, as from bold eagles thine,
Comes name of Columbine.

FIELD SPARROW.

Shy little mother bird with beating heart,
  With anxious thought for those she loves the best,
This thin grass threading with deceptive art
To lead my dread, intruding steps apart
  From her fond treasure cowering in the nest!

Thou hast no heart to sing whilst danger's near,
  Nor chirp or cry of pain escapes thy throat,
But let me draw aside and I shall hear
A low-trilled melody how soft and clear!
  A soul's deep tenderness in every note!

Thou keepest close the secret of thy breast,
  Shared with thy mate and with thy mate alone,
The spot where lie those dear ones in the nest,
Nor from thy movements can the place be guessed —
  To but one other faithful Watcher known!

KINGCUPS.

When knights were gathered at King Arthur's court
    The chivalry, the peerage of the land,
Keen to display their skill at knightly sport
    For prize of gilded belt, of princess' hand;
At banquet met around the royal board,
    That table round by Merlin made of old,
For king and knight rich, ruddy wine was poured.
    A purple drink, in cup of yellow gold.

Ye golden cups on Spring's fair meadows green
    Are kingcups fit to grace a fairy board,
Held high in dainty hand of fairy queen,
    Titania's hand, to pledge her fairy lord;
Unsoiled ye are by any stain or blot
    From blood of mortal man in battle slain,
Your wine the morning dew that blushes not
    At any fancy bred in fairy brain.

Your pliant stalks bend under passing breeze,
    Ye lout and curtesy to the sun above,
He sips that proffered beverage to the lees,
    Gives back gold bright as that which misers love.
We watch your glittering cups made all aglow
    With living splendor on these festal days,
From that rich pearly offering we know
    What courtly homage generous Nature pays.

43

ORIOLE.

When Flora's handmaids throw
Over the orchard branches bare
A robe of pink and white so fair
    It rivals winter's snow,
Then cherry blossoms give to sight,
Their purity of unstained white,
Then in the pink upon the apple tree,
So delicate and soft, we faintly see
    Fore-gleams of summer's glow.

Then do we fondly dream
Of golden sunlight on the hills,
Of laughter rippling from the rills,
    Of lilies on the stream;
Then squirrels racing without care,
Gay insects dancing in the air,
The low sweet song of Nature softly heard,
Crooned over lovingly by bee and bird,
    A present rapture seem.

While we are lost in thought,
Or lost in wonder and surprise
At beauty opening to our eyes
    By Spring's fair heralds brought,
Are lost in dreams of loveliness
Beyond our power to express,
Upon a sudden, startlingly, behold!
A flashing gleam of crimson and of gold
    Our wondering sight has caught.

From lands where all the year
The sun burns with untempered glow,
Where day by day the flowers blow
    Nor cold of winter fear;
From groves made fair with orange bloom
And scented with that rich perfume,
While barely yet in Northern pine and fir
Do currents of the sap begin to stir,
    The oriole is here!

PANSIES.

For gentle thought
Of all things innocent and good
In garden growing or in planted field,
In orchard or in wood;
For gentle thought of plant and shrub that yield
Their fragrance to the desert spot,
The beauty of their blossoms for delight
Of our enraptured sight,
Their sweet and mellow - ripened fruit for food!

For kindly thought
Of fellow creatures on the earth,
Down in the grasses, up among the trees,
Their home their place of birth;
For kindly thought of birds that sing and bees
Late coming home with burdens sought
From flowers opening on shrub and tree
While sing the birds with glee
To waken in our hearts their joy and mirth!

For happy thought
Of friends, the absent and the near,
Who watch, as we, the blossom and the bird,
Who listen hushed to hear
The songs which in their childhood days they heard
In well - remembered spot
Where stood together with them listening long
To chirp, or trill, or song,
Companions in their joys and griefs most dear!

SONG SPARROW.

A few notes, three or four,
Repeated o'er and o'er
  In low, soft, liquid strains,
Make all thy hymn of praise,
Sing all love's tender lays,
  Sing even love's sweet pains.

Thy fond mate sitting near
Is glad as I to hear
  That triumph of thine art;
Just that same song of thine,
Sung over line by line,
  Won her grandmother's heart.

APPLE BLOSSOMS.

Stripped of their leaves and bare
  Have stood the apple trees all winter long
  Uncheered by sparrow's song
Or kingbird hovering noisy in the air
  Above its wool-lined nest,
Guarding its twittering young with jealous care
Against marauding hawk that bold would dare
  Its orchard home molest.

Their trunks with moss o'ergrown,
  All gnarled and seamed and knotted by the storm,
  With little grace of form,
But lichen-robed in hues of richest tone
  They stand in sturdy row,
Their naked boughs as sinewy arms upthrown ·
Against the winter's sky, or clad alone
  In ice and soft white snow.

This warm sweet summer's day,
  A foretaste of what waits for us in June, ·
  The orioles are in tune,
The lilac boughs with purple bloom are gay;
  And in the morning light
The apple trees that looked so old and gray,
So bare of beauty in this beauteous May,
  Stand robed in pink and white!

The vision of delight
  Sends Fancy roving where the fair earth lies
  Beneath enchanting skies,
All fields and hedges decked with flowers bright,
  With ripening fruits as well:—
There in a garden pleasant to the sight
Man with his Maker walked in his own right;
  Ah, that he ever fell!

Or Fancy, seeing these
  Sweet blossoms kindred to the blushing rose
  That by the wayside grows,
Is hurried on to lands beyond the seas,
  To gardens in the west
Where, watching golden apples on the trees,
Dwell evermore the fair Hesperides
  In Islands of the Blest.

VEERY.

Soon as the gray of morn begins to break
  Through leaden border of dim eastern skies,
Rathe Hours lead up the day, the dull clouds take
  The tincture of the morning's saffron dyes;
Take forms of grace as for Aurora's sake
  Did incense from her flaming altars rise;
Then happy birds from dreamless slumbers wake
And in the hush of silent nature make
  A symphony of their sweet melodies.

Soon as the hasting sun goes down at night,
  His journey of the day brought to its close,
The brilliancy and glory of his light
  Intense upon the clouds above he throws;
Beneath those curtain folds so soft, so bright,
  A world of tired birds sinks to repose,
Fond hearts of young o'erflowing with delight,
Sad hearts of old with care o'erburdened quite
  In lullabies forget their joys, their woes.

First is the veery of that tuneful choir
  His voice in morning anthem sweet to raise,
When, too, the evening shades are drawing nigher
  He is the last to close his simple lays!
No sweeter note gives out Apollo's lyre,
  None sweeter gives the shell his brother plays;
This gift of tawny thrush transcends the fire
Of any mortal soul that would aspire
  To sing—as now I sing—the veery's praise.

BUTTERCUPS.

Through the meadows running
  Crowfoot tracks are seen,
With the crow's deep cunning
  Hidden in the green;
Who would guess their warning,
  Who would stop to think,
Finding them this morning
  By the runnel's brink?

Crowfoot tracks in legion
  Running all about
Show this favored region
  Has seen a merry rout;
Here have housewife fairies,
  With fairy swain and maid,
Set up summer dairies
  In the plantain's shade.

Tender cowslips over
  Breathes a fragrance sweet
From the scented clover
  Fairy heifers eat;
Milkworts shyly living
  With primrose and with fern,
Golden cream are giving
  For the fairies' churn.

Come when birds are singing
  Early in the morn,
While the dew is clinging
  To the blades of corn,
You shall see each fairy,
  Standing tiptoe, hold
Product of her dairy
  In buttercup of gold.

JENNIE WREN.

In early spring we hear you sing
   The old, the well-remembered song
Sung o'er and o'er in years before,
   Forgotten not in winters long;
As in and out, and all about
   The rural homes of lonely men,
Your presence near brings added cheer
   To April's sun, sweet Jennie Wren.

For dainty crumb you fearless come
   To open window for your food,
To set the child with wonder wild,
   To rouse up puss with thirst for blood,
Safe in your skill to turn at will
   As sunbeam flashed from mirror bright,
Poor puss you tease just as you please,
   Then have you disappeared from sight.

All summer long your cheery song
   Was heard from yard and garden nigh,
From early light till when at night
   The veery sung her lullaby;
That song denied, at Christmas-tide
   Our thoughts go back to summer when
With hum of bees round cherry trees
   Was heard sweet voice of Jennie Wren.

LADY'S SLIPPER.

Whose dainty foot
Once wore in maiden pride
This unlaced slipper wrought in pink and white
Left here in sudden flight
At this pine's root
Upon the streamlet's side?
Or was it cast away
By dryad, nymph, or fay,
When she was overcome and dazed by panic fright?

It swings and nods
Upon that slender stalk
As if its owner had but just now fled;
Could she have heard us tread
On spongy sods,
Or overheard our talk
As we came down the brook
Minding our line and hook,
Careful that timid trout should not be seized with dread?

Or did she spy
The wolf's-foot painted green
In trailing moss upon the shaded ground,
Soft creeping all around
Cautious and shy
As prowling wolf is seen?
Did she consult her fear,
Deeming the danger near,
And leave her loosened slipper at the first light bound?

NUTHATCH.

Up and down the maples rough and shaggy-coated,
  Busy searching through the lichens all the day,
Shyly creeps the tiny nuthatch snowy-throated,
  Sharply eyeing every crevice for its prey;
In and out along the boughs with gray moss covered,
  Gnarled and knotted in their struggles with the
      storm,
Through the mass of tender leafage is discovered
  Here and there about its work that slender form.

Pleasant 'tis for us to watch our cheerful neighbor
  Happy in the work of caring for its brood,
Finding only joy and comfort in its labor,
  Winning for its little ones their daily food;
Pleasant 'tis to think that when the snow is flying,
  When the leaves are gone and gone the summer bird,
Up among the frozen branches creaking, crying,
  This same note of sweet contentment will be heard.

BARBERRY.

On rocky hillside pastures growing wild
  By sufferance of man, not with his care,
Among the broken ledges, boulders piled
  In menacing disorder here and there,
  Has fled the barberry bush as to its lair
Flees hunted creature of the wilderness
  Before the fierce pursuer with his hound,
Its faint heart beating wildly in distress
  To hear the barking dogs, the bugle's sound.

Here has the barberry a refuge found,
  A desert stronghold for its safety made,
Has taken weapons sharp wherewith to wound
  Whoever may its chosen spot invade,
  Each stem and leaf thick set with point and blade:
For war equipped it hangs in early spring
  Defiant flag of gold o'er castle wall,
In softer mood entices with a string
  Of beaded coral later in the fall.

ON BOBOLINK GROUND.

Here will the meadow lark be found
　Near neighbor to the bobolink,
Joint owners they of low wet ground
　That lies along the river's brink,
Where thick the alder bushes grow,
Where willows swing their branches low,
　Of running stream to drink.

Here violets in the mowing field
　Wake early from their winter's nest,
Here tufted grasses spring to shield
　Weak fledglings chirping in the nest;
Gay grow the fields with orchids rare,
With crane's-bill and with crowfoot fair;
　Here sing the birds their best.

Could man have brought from regions fair
　Whence angels led him to his birth,
Gifts that with wild notes could compare,
　With song of birds of equal worth;
A gift like theirs the sense to please,
To charm the soul, the heart to ease,
　Then might he own the earth.

MEADOW CRANE'S-BILL.

Through meadows green
The tiny streamlet, wandering idly, goes
With many a winding turn
Between its banks of fern,
Or clumps of hardhack growth and wilding rose
In blossom seen.

Now blowing sweet
From over strawberry beds, through clustered grove
Of flowering basswood trees,
Loved haunt of humming bees,
As idle as the brook the breezes rove
On sandalled feet.

Lithe grasses low
Bend down in reverence as the breezes pass:
The fern frond easy swings
As swallow on his wings
Turns in his rapid flight and skims the grass
As shadows go.

In noble pride
The orchis holds his purple head high up
Above tho violets shy
That in the grasses lie,
Outrivalling tho golden buttercup
Close by his side.

These nodding greet
Tho gentle crane's-bill living o'er the way;
Well-bred the comely race
That with bewitching grace
The compliments of buttercups repay
With courtesy sweet.

VIREO.

What soft notes ringing clear,
What sweet strain do we hear
  Sung to melodious tune
From out the elm tops high,
Outlined against the sky
  Of this bright day in June?

Fierce beats the noontide sun,
But rippling waters run,
  Song led, from shaded pool;
Blithe naiads trip along
To the measure of that song
  Heard from the shadows cool;

Or is it that the bird
A naiad's step has heard,
  Has caught its rhythmic beat?
Is that the secret known
To one blest bird alone
  To make its song so sweet?

PRIMROSE.

The sun is down,—his latest lingering beams
  Swept from far western hills their crown of gold,
They took the shimmering light from off the streams:
The burnished gold that from the kingcup gleams
  Green sepals close enfold.

The moon is up,—through limbs of ash trees dead
  She peers across the dusky wooded land,
On clover bloom the winds more lightly tread,
The drowsy poppy nods and droops her head,
  Her flame more lightly fanned.

The laden bee, surprised while homeward bound,
  Belated by his greed, holds on his way;
His droning hum low blends with pensive sound
Of home-fast cricket chirping on the ground
  To while the hours away.

Soft sleeps the daisy by the sparrow's nest,
  The firefly flickers over meadows damp,
Low chirping thrushes, 'neath their mother's breast,
With her sweet lullaby are hushed to rest:—
  Pale primrose lights her lamp.

Bright yellow buttercup at summer's noon
  Returns the sun more than he gives of gold,
So does the primrose, with her lavish boon,
Burn softer flame than does the tender moon,—
  Shines with a ray less cold.

VESPERS AND MATINS.

Soft and slow,
Faint and low,
Sings the hermit thrush her evening lullaby;
On a birch twig swinging,
To her loved ones singing,
Swinging,
Singing,
Softer yet and slower,
Fainter yet and lower,
Ring the bell-like notes till all the echoes die,
Till the hush of slumbers
Drowns the drowsy numbers,
Till the sleep of sacred silence seals the weary
watcher's eye.

Soon as light
Follows night,
Coursing all the lands and waters o'er,
With the day's first breaking,
From their slumbers waking, —
Cheep, cheep;
Peep, peep, —
In a burst of gladness,
Of ecstatic madness,
All the birds together their songs of greeting pour,
Pour their souls in singing
Till the woods are ringing
Just as if on eastern borders day had never dawned
before.

SUN DEW.

The soil beneath our feet,
Along the brook-side in the mowing field,
Is soft and springy, — downy mosses yield
To lightest pressure; where our feet have set
A deep mould in low bended grasses wet,
    Rise waters cool and sweet.

From all the leaves around,
From stalk and stem, from blade and flower cup
The sun has drunk the dew of morning up;
The purple orchis proudly lifts its head,
Blue violets lie sleepy in their bed,
    In dreamy slumber drowned.

Here sun dew in the moss
Stretches its leaf-stalks as extended arms,
Holds to the heavens its broad, round, upturned palms
Brimmed with the crystal drops its leaves distill,
Begs the hot noontide sunbeam drink its fill,
    Nor suffers any loss.

WHITE-THROATED SPARROW.

How sweet that singing heard
From thicket fringing round the shadowy wood
Close bordering the field of ripening corn !
    'Tis the white-throated bird.
The wren-like sparrow, singing plaintive song,
Low calling lovingly, in tender mood,
    His mate away so long.
How have I listened to that longing cry !
"Madam Peabody, Peabody, Peabody, why
    Tarry you all the morn ?"

The summer noon is still,
Save cricket's chirping in the yellowing grain
Blends with the hum of honey-gathering bees,
    In concert faint but shrill.
The butterfly goes past on noiseless wing:
And now I hear in melody again
    The lonely sparrow sing,
Low chanting over that same song alway,
"Madam Peabody, Peabody, Peabody, pray,
    Hurry back home, do, please."

LAUREL.

Under the winter's snow
　　All flashing, sparkling white,
　　　　With ice thick crusted o'er,
　　　　With rime and frost-work hoar
　　And crystals shining bright,
Long leaves of laurel show
　　As soft, as tender, green
　　As when in summer seen
Beneath the hot sun all aglow
　　On pastured slope, on mountain height,
　　　　Gray granite ledges hung before
　　　　To curtain those with velvet sheen.

Now with a softer white
　　Than any Winter knows,
　　　　Just tinted with the flush
　　　　Of a half-conscious blush
　　As borrowed from the rose,
Comes laurel to our sight.
　　　　Pranked out in such array
　　　　It seems the fair one may
Have met elves on midsummer's night;
　　This work of Nature's weaving throws
　　　　Such witchery on rock and bush
　　　　We know not what to think or say.

NIGHT HAWK.

Silent of voice and wing,
  Low brooding all the day
  On bare rock lichened gray,
You hear the thickets ring
With songs the thrushes sing,
  Unheeding all the wood's glad life at play.

As motionless as stone,
  All mottled brown and white
  Your form deceives the sight;
It seems that life has flown,
That flesh and blood have grown
  Into the semblance of gray granite quite;

Until the step is nigh
  Of one whose eager quest
  For Nature's thought is pressed,
Then with a whimpering cry,
As broken-winged, you fly
  Or flutter helpless from your guarded nest.

Not yet does Nature quite
  Her secret drawer unlock;
  Still do the round eggs mock
The intruder's keenest sight,
For, speckled brown and white,
  These match the gray tone of the naked rock.

Without a stick to hedge
  The bare home spot around,
  The lonely nest is found
Upon the hard, sharp edge
Of a sun-beaten ledge
  That crops out in the open pasture ground.

MOUSE-EAR CHICKWEED.

Dearest but humblest born
Of Nature's blameless brood,
Creeping among the grass, among the corn,
Keeping well out of sight,
Beneath the dock and plantain hidden quite,
Sleeping in bivouac through the summer's night
Around the glow-worm's light,
Poor gipsy vagabond of road and lane,
Thou hast of men their coldness and disdain,
Contempt and bitter scorn:
Yet mother Nature, good
To all her children with unstinted love,
Holds thy form closely pressed
To her warm loving breast,
And smiles in sunshine on thy frequent bloom.
Brighter the world to thee
Than to the laurel tree
Brought from the dank depths of the forest gloom,
Only a prize to be
To grace a victory,
Or, mimicking bowed Sorrow, lean above
Red-handed conqueror sleeping in his tomb.

WHIPPOORWILL.

One by one the voices of the daytime
  Cease their prattle at the evening hour,
Weary with the pleasures of their playtime
  Little birds are resting in their bower;
One by one their hymns of praise are chanted,
  Brought to a lapsing close in evensong,
In the silent night the wood is haunted
  By a mournful cry repeated long.
    Deeper grow the shadows
    On the fields and meadows;
Sinking low or rising high,
Shining far or flashing nigh,
Lights her lamp the firefly.
    Round the silent mill,
    In the evening still,
Up the rill, down the rill,
Wanders weary Echo crying still
"Whip-poor-Will! Whip-poor-Will!"

Now the long bright summer's day is ended,
    Faded wholly from the earth and sky,
Clover field and wooded slope are blended
    In one mass of purple to the eye:
All alone, more lonely for that crying,
    From the distant wood or orchard near,
Echo, busy to that voice replying,
    Sad the cry repeats in accents clear.
        Nearer sounds the flowing
        Of the mill-stream going
Down its bed with broken fall,
Tumbling over rocks and all;
With its roar is heard the call
        Mingling with the trill
        Of the tree-toad shrill.
Up the hill, down the hill
Wanders weary Echo crying still,
"Whip-poor-Will! "Whip-poor-Will!"

WATER LILIES.

Beneath the shadows cold
Of broken ledges old,
High towering, sheer and bold,
Against the smiling field of summer's blue,
Where, every morning, climbs the sun anew
The mystic golden staircase leading through
Vast upward curling fold
Of gray mist softly rolled
From off the water's face,—the still lake lies,
Calm, clear and blue as noon-tide's cloudless skies.

All watching for the light,
Still in the shade of night
The royal lilies white
Their close shut petals slowly now unfold,
Displaying to the day the wealth they hold,
A golden altar with its flame of gold,
All glowing warm and bright
To fascinate the sight,
And breathing out a fragrance as divine
As is frankincense on Apollo's shrine.

MEADOW LARK.

The breeze that faintest fragrance brings
  From hardhack, fern, and thistle,
Bears song of meadow lark that sings
  With low and plaintive whistle;
Above the dusty stubble ground,
  The thicket's leafy cover,
Wide pasture-waste, sun-burnt and browned,
  Shy larks, shrill piping, hover.

While yet the snow lies on the hill
  We greet this early comer,
We neighbor with it gladly till
  We've said "Good-bye!" to summer.
How many a morning of July,
  When in the meadow mowing,
I've listened to that timid cry
  Heard with the cock's bold crowing!

IRIS.

Above the plashy pool,
With pond-weed growing in close neighborhood
And standing knee-deep in the stagnant flood.
    Beneath the sun's hot rays
    At noon of summer days,
Fair, languid Iris droops her head, and dreams
Of harebells overhanging laughing streams
    Up on the mountains cool.

    The meadow all around
Is soft with moss and grasses growing green,
Here lilies, jonquils, crocuses are seen,
    All flowers growing best
    Where silent waters rest;
Foundation these from which the arches rise
To span with splendid hues the weeping skies; —
    Here pot of gold is found!

    By that fair, shining way,
Came Iris once down from Olympus high,
She marked with light her course across the sky,
    And still it shows as plain,
    Fresh washed with falling rain,
As if the maid of Juno took her flight
Back from the earth to that celestial height
    Where it is noon for aye.

BARN SWALLOWS.

I have in mind a farmstead 'mong the hills,
A broken region rich in ponds and rills,
With mountain ranges on the north and west,
Upon the south, a lonely lake at rest;
The farm itself a ridge of easy slope,
    With dark old forest growth on either side,
Its fields and pastures offering generous scope
    For oxen ploughing, cattle ranging wide:
Those fields and pastures fenced with walls of stone,
Gray boulders with gray lichens overgrown;
The rising summit of the long ridge crowned
With low farm - buildings weather - worn and browned,
With orchard trees close clustering around.

I have in mind a barn extending wide,
With low - roofed sheds attached on either side,
Their eaves, projecting, offered tempting seat
For nests of swallows, ranged as on a street;
Adobe - built, these seemed to wondering eyes
    That watched for years that street's increasing
        length,
That saw its walls by swallow labor rise,
    As if 'twere built of Cyclopean strength,
But underneath those ample sheds, storm - proof,
Within the barn, beneath its spacious roof,
Wherever rib or rafter furnished rest,
Was built of mud and straw a swallow's nest
For brood in Continental colors dressed.

Swift over fields of clover, skimming low,
The eager swallows hurry to and fro;
With easy grace they turn, they sink, they rise,
To catch the white-winged miller as it flies.
A sweetly simple melody they sing,
    With friendly note the barefoot boy they greet,
While plying brisk their foray on the wing,
    They circle round the wondering urchin's feet;
But when the parent birds come home with food,
The barn is bedlam with the noisy brood.
Each year such care the swallow's time employs
To still, to hush the summer's twittering noise; —
Ghosts of their youth as men are ghosts of boys.

ORCHIS.

Deep in moist meadows with fair iris growing,
  Where blossomed buttercups in early May,
Its spike of purple flowers proudly showing,
  The orchis holds its head high up to-day.

It stands breast-high among the bending grasses
  That with the summer breezes rise and sink,
Loads with its fragrance every breath that passes,
  Though burdened this with song of bobolink.

At dawn it sends this winsome message over
  To call afield the bees and butterflies,
Above the billowy seas of purple clover
  This eager horde of honey-seekers hies.

They find the orchis, in its stately beauty,
  As picket stationed here some charge to keep,
Alert, devoted to its sacred duty,
  To guard the spot where tender fledglings sleep.

Above that helmet plumed, and worn so proudly,
  On fluttering wing hangs anxious bobolink;
He greets his waiting home by singing loudly,
  With cadence of his song at last to sink.

CEDAR BIRD.

Trig, natty little fop,
  The prince of feathered beaux,
At home in cedar's top
  Or in the orchard close;
With equal neatness dressed
In ashy-olive vest,
Whether in sunshine bright or dismal storm
We note your simple taste, your comely form.

With well-becoming grace
  You wear your jaunty crest,
With pertness in your face
  Come an unbidden guest;
Your friends you bring to eat
Our cherries ripe and sweet
As if it were for you and yours alone
That in our gardens cherries red are grown.

With joy you hail the sight
  Of cherries growing red,
You watch with keen delight
  The crimson blushes spread,
While not a blush we trace
On your provoking face
All radiant with eagerness and haste
The quality of ox-heart fruit to taste.

WOOD-SORREL.

Upon the sloping bank of woodland stream,
Fair as a fairy's dream,
Wakes nymph Wood-Sorrel, opening wide her eyes
To Spring's low-arching skies;
Its leaves,—as many as the Graces—seen
At evening golden-green,
Will in the morning light display with pride
Their purple under side,
Worn as the royal purple of the East
To grace a royal feast,
Embroidered either side in lines as fair
As locks of maiden's hair.

Heart-shaped each tiny leaf that we may know
The tender thought below,
That springs to meet us in the blossoms sweet
Low bowing at our feet;
On slender stems of pink and green they swing
As birds upon the wing,
Their white-empurpled petals worn as gay
As crown by Queen of May,
In numbers gathering to this quiet nook
Beside the plashy brook,
They deck this mossy bank beneath the firs
For Flora's worshippers.

SWAMP SPARROW.

Along the sloping edge
  Of clover fields red - blossoming in June,
Where butterflies and bees together come
  To fill the air with beauty and with sound,
    Till all the place around
Is hushed to quiet by a murmurous hum,
There grow the hazels thickest in the hedge
There dogwood blossomed in the early Spring;
  The briers keep the barefoot boy away
Though in the swamp he hears a shy bird sing
    A wonderful sweet tune,
Though to his ears the notes melodious ring
  As if 'twere Orpheus with his strings at play.

A breath of incense sweet
  Is breathed from twin - flowers growing in the moss
That trails along the hemlock half - decayed,
  High up in tops of whispering pines and firs
    The soft breeze lightly stirs
Their balsam boughs till melody is made,
Then does the low trill of the sparrow greet
The listening ear of deep - enchanted boy
  Who, wondering, holds his breath and listens long,
Thrilled, as the trees are thrilled, with rapturous joy,
    Impatient of the loss
Of single note sung by that minstrel coy; —
  Himself lost in the mystery of song.

SWEET CLOVER.

As wild thyme, on the slopes of Hybla growing,
   Was fed upon by honey-loving bees,
Soft airs Sicilian from the mountain blowing
   Sweet perfume wafted far out on the seas;
So in our lanes, through fields and meadows going,
   Where clasp the pleading buttercups our knees,
White clover springs from Nature's kindly sowing,
   Rich fragrance breathing on the passing breeze.

New England's snow-clad hills this winter's morning
   With slopes of Sicily but ill compare,
Our fields wear only white for their adorning
   While thyme and cytisus are growing there;
Let but the breath of June steal softly over
   Our summer landscape clothed in beauty rare,
Then will the perfume of sweet-scented clover
   Tempt honey-hoarding misers to despair.

BLUE HERON.

Low down the western sky
  Rests setting sun on mountain's burning ridge
    As if his tired steeds
    Were here turned loose to graze rich lotus
      meads,
In evening peace, that lie
Beyond the utmost reach of mortal eye;
  His slant rays span with golden bridge
The broad low valley with its darkening stream,
  Whose silent reaches under giant pines
  In shadow slumber while the low sun shines
Upon those lofty tops with good-night beam.

Slow coming into view
  From out the fleecy clouds of vapor rolled
    From sea on eastern side,
    A small dark speck is suddenly descried
Against the deepening blue:
It grows upon the vision as they grew,
  Those coming ships we watched of old.
Against the arrowy beams flashed from the west
  The heron wings her way with daily food,
  Filched from the sea, to feed her hungry brood
Left, 'mong the pine tops, in a lonely nest.

An open space
Of almost naked rock,
Of ledges rounded into billowy forms
Like those that heave upon the Atlantic's breast,
That, shoreward driven by storms,
Roll in on Swampscot Beach with swelling crest,
Till, checked their race,
They break with thundering shock;
So lie Lynn Commons, bleak and bare,
With only here and there
In some deep-sheltered nook
Grown round by alders low,
By swamp-pink blossoming like snow,
A little crystal pool
Of waters fresh and cool,
Fed by the tribute of a slender brook,
To whose green side
Sweet clover blossoms tempt the wandering bees,
Where, in lithe elms and spreading willow trees,
Do wren and thrush all summer long abide.

These sloping sides
Of glacier - polished ledge,
As if, in some far - distant age unknown,
These had been smoothed as rocks upon the shore
Of an ice - burdened zone,
Their rounded surface barely covered o'er
With strip of soil that hides
Scant border round their edge, —
A soil as thin and poor
As that on English moor
Washed down by winter rains,
Too scanty soil to bear
A forest growth, but everywhere
Low savin bushes keep
Firm hold in crevice deep
Beside the purple porphyritic veins.
Here fairies tread,
Hither among the moss the cinque - foil creeps,
With jealous lichens gray it firmly keeps
A miser's clutch upon its rocky bed.

Through misty haze
We look upon this rugged scene, —
This bit of Old World landscape in the New —
At early morning in the month of June;
The sun drinks up the dew,
But notes are lacking from the siren tune
Heard on such days
In fields and woodlands green;
We wonder at the change,
The scene presents a strange,
But rapturous, aspect to our sight!
What harmony doth show
Of light above, of gold below,
As if had Nature tried
The naked rock to hide
With filmy folds of saffron-colored light!
She weaves us here
With most consummate skill a splendid shroud,
Warm fabric of the sunbeam and the cloud,
Veiling her features hard with smile and tear.

So gray and cold
Were ledges bare and steep
Before the wild flowers wakened to the light,
Roused by the coming of the year's bright day
After its winter night!
Dreamed these of tones in color, forms bedight
With burnished gold,
In their unbroken sleep?
Of coquetry of light and shade,
Arch nod to passing maid,
Of banners borne afield
Above high - waving crest,
Above long ranks of gallant men abreast?
Or was it with surprise
This splendor met their eyes,
Flashed from the ledge as from a golden shield?
O banneret
Unfurled of richest golden - petalled bloom,
Of yellow - flowered, heath - enamored broom
Worn in the cap of the Plantagenet!

Our souls with awe
Are bowed before the sight
Of so much beauty on the landscape thrown,
Such wealth of color used with lavish hand
On cold, gray granite stone,
Until this lone spot rivals any land
Eyes ever saw
Beneath the heaven's broad light,
Until we come to realize
The rapture and surprise
With which Linnœus found
Himself, that day in June
When thrush and linnet were in tune,
Delighted with the sight
Of golden broom flowers bright
Clothing a barren waste of English ground.
Low kneeling there
Upon that stretch of richly colored sod
He raised his voice in thankfulness to God
For having made a world so bright and fair.

As now we gaze
On yellow-tufted broom,
We see this stranger plant, of foreign stock,
Clinging to this one lone and rugged spot,
This naked barren rock,
Now are we carried back in pondering thought
To earlier days
When this bright bit of bloom
Our fathers and our mothers bore
From England's pleasant shore
To plant in their new home,
That, as it spread and grew,
Its sight might link the Old World to the New;
That it might blossom here
At noontide of the year
As it had bloomed on Surrey's chalky loam.
Its beauty told,
When petals opened with their burning glow
And lighted up this waste with brilliant show,
Affection's bonds were bright as chains of gold.

We look away,
Far off upon the sea,
Beyond the outline of this broken shore;
So does our eager fancy strive to press
From when our sires came o'er
From mother England to this wilderness.
In that far day
On Gallic field we see
Proud Henry wearing badge of broom,
Vailed at à Becket's tomb,
But shining in the fray.
And him we see, whose name
Brought fear to man and brute where'er he came,
The lion - hearted one,
Leading Crusaders on
To victory beneath this yellow spray.
Our fancies go
On wayward wanderings, and back they bring
Some thought of Geoffrey, Anjou's noble king,
Of those who sleep with him at Fontevrault.

WARBLING GREENLET.

Still fall the rain-drops through the birch leaves
   tender,
  With motion tremulous,, with rippling sound,
They steal along the smooth twigs lithe and slender,
   To fall on withered leaves that strew the ground;
Through rifts in ragged storm-clouds rent and
   broken,
  Pour down the golden sunbeams bright and warm,
They thread the lines of rain and set the token
  Of ancient covenant on passing storm.
Down through the birch leaves, with the rain-drops
   falling,
  Come liquid strains of simplest melody,
Sweet, cheerful note of happy greenlet calling
  To kindred songster in the neighbor tree;
The frowning cloud with glorious splendor lighted
  In speechless rapture holds entrancéd gaze, —
Let greenlet's tones, with sound of leaves united,
  Now weave for us a fitting hymn of praise!

SWAMP PINK.

The maiden's happiness,
Which she for worlds on worlds would not confess
The world can rightly guess
From merry song that sings itself to-day;
Let her contrive all art
Her every look and movement will betray
The secret of her heart.

The flower, opening pale
On wilding shrub, its sweetness must exhale
To breath of passing gale;
Though envious brambles clamber to conceal
The modest blushing face,
Her breath of sweetest fragrance will reveal
The Swamp Pink's lowly place.

SWALLOW'S FLIGHT.

Glad greeting give we in the spring
When, in surprise, we hear you sing
Or see the glancing of a wing
    Round low eaves overjutting;
'Neath shingle edge and water spout
Ye gather, flitting in and out
Your clay-built homes thick set about,
    On beam and plate abutting.

In empty loft of barn and shed,
Above the unused cart and sled,
In summers past your young were bred
    With not one thought of danger.
Content with your domestic joys,
The tease of puss, delight of boys,
Ye filled the spacious barn with noise
    That drowned the low from manger.

O swallow, at the early light
The mower marked thy rapid flight,
That dipping of the wings so slight
    With which thou crossed the ocean.
How well do I remember thee
Thus darting by in front of me,
And in that rhythmic flight I see
    The poetry of motion.

PITCHER-PLANT.

Once was a modern fancy tempted fair
By ancient Grecian urn of beauty rare,
Whose well proportioned form had potter graced
With glad procession, round the border traced;
The lovely maiden's beauty ne'er should fade,
The eager lover never win the maid;
So had the artist to his fancy wrought,
So shaped to this far age his happiest thought!
Henceforth that urn its round of years repeats
Accompanied by gracious thought of Keats.

To-day these pitchers, wrought to Nature's mind
In lonely wood-surrounded spot I find,
Their forms as perfect and unchanged they hold
As potter's work preserved from days of old;
So curls the lip about the outer rim,
So stands the water even with the brim,
So are they painted by the summer sun,
In brown and purple tints the colors run,
Fronds blend with vines except where mosses
        hide
A patch of green upon the under side.

PHOEBE.

Who hears that note of call
  For Phoebe in the spring?
From garden fence, or wall,
From sloping well-sweep tall
    The cries repeated ring;—
    Soon will the summons bring
The bird beloved of all.

Still, "Phoebe!" do we hear,
    Called from the orchard tree
In accents loud and clear;
When will the bird appear?
    Calling impatiently
    When shall the fond mate see
The housewife, Phoebe, here?

Here is the last year's nest
    'Twas Phoebe's happy home,
Of workmanship the best,
With silken fibers dressed,
    Fair as a palace dome:
    Again shall Phoebe come
Again will it be blest.

Ah, Phoebe, Phoebe, you
    Are really staying late!
Nay, this will never do,
To slight a love so true!
    Already is your mate
    Made quite disconsolate,
And we are waiting, too.

CLEMATIS.

Climbing over walls and hedges,
Clambering over rocks and ledges,
Runs at large the wilding clematis as a truant
    child at play;
Hand in hand with clinging bramble,
Boon companions both, these ramble
Over ditches by the roadside, all along the dusty
    way.

Through the fields and through the meadows,
In the sun and in the shadows,
On dry bank and springy brookside equally this
    wilding grows;
Through the fences and through bushes
Where the sparrows and shy thrushes
Hide from sight their precious nestlings, there this
    fearless runner goes.

Over sagging rails decaying,
Up the stakes but feebly staying,
Where the playful squirrels scamper, run and chat-
ter in their play;
Filling all the gaps and breaches
With its long and swaying reaches,
Grows the vigorous young clematis concealing old
decay.

In an earlier age, when Beauty
Owed to Use not any duty,
When our fathers looked upon the world with the
feelings of a boy;
Then they saw why roads were haunted
By this graceful runner planted
By the bounteous hand of Nature, and they called
it Traveler's Joy.

THRUSH'S LULLABY.

When the days in summer die,
When the light fades from the sky,
    Then the thrush
    In the bush
Sings her evening lullaby;
Then the stars that are so high,
Winking roguishly and sly
    To the stars that dance and shiver
    On the ripples of the river
    As the leaves of poplars quiver
When the summer breeze goes by,
Wink and nod to primrose shy
As she opens wide her eye,
Waking with the firefly
    From her day-dreams fair and bright
    To the glories of the night,
Just when lilies on the stream
Close their drowsy eyes to dream
    Of the glories of the day.
    How with steady gaze do they
        Every one
        Watch the sun
    From the dawn till evening gray,
    Till his splendors die away!
When the darkness brooding nigh
Silences each twittering cry
        To a hush,
        Then the thrush
        In the bush
Leads to a lapsing close her low-trilled lullaby.

TWIN - FLOWER.

O strangely rare!
The odor faint brought on the passing breeze,
The balsam breath blown from the tall fir trees
    That silent rise and fair,
    In the hot summer air!

And, mingling sweet,
A rich perfume, more delicate by far
Than spicy gales from tropic islands are,
    Rises about our feet,
    For offered incense meet.

Beneath the screen
Of bearded hemlock boughs and royal pines,
The twin-flower traces with its slender vines
    A pattern dimly seen
    On carpet soft and green.

The springy moss
Retains slight impress of the trampling foot,
But thick on fallen trunk and buttress root
    Slowly it creeps across
    Decay, and hides all loss.

But here and there
A delicate pale flower turns its head
To sweetheart's kiss; — more softly now we tread,
    By fragrance made aware
    Of the fond loving pair.

YELLOW BIRD.

Erect, alone,
Alert as picket on the outer line,
Amid a waste of sands,
Or posted by a stone
With lichens overgrown
On hill-side sheepwalk under August's shine,
The stately mullein stands,
Craving no part in lands
To drought unknown.
About its feet are seen
Soft robes of velvet green
In which its early youth was richly dressed,
Now upward from the waist
On lines that run oblique across its breast,
At intervals are decorations placed,
Mild stars of softest gold,
Such gold as waking primroses unfold,
To Venus shining bright, and low down in the west.

Well poised is worn
A burnished helmet of that self-same gold
With which its sides are graced;
As martial, is it sworn,
As Roman eagle borne
By legionary troops through Gaul of old,
Or royal standard placed
On Syria's desert waste,
Unawed, untorn;
Till easy as a thought
By sudden fancy caught
This Phrygian symbol takes its flight so free,
Now falling and anon
Rising with gentle grace as billows on the sea,
To yonder ripening thistle is it gone,
And as it floats along
It times the rhythmic movements with its
song;
Exultant mounts each crest, with soft *che-wee, che-wee!*

YARROW.

In close companionship with man
    Yet having in his thought no share,
      A poor neglected weed,
Outcast, existing under ban,
    Unheeded vagrant everywhere
      That human footsteps lead,
By dusty road, green lane and footpath narrow,
Grows with its thousand feathery leaves the yarrow.

In God's great, universal plan,
    Of our poor notice, of our care
      The milfoil hath what need?
Those leaves, so softly bending, can
    Show service in the world as fair
      As is man's noblest deed; —
In Spring-time down the lane the social sparrow
Builds trustingly her nest 'neath sheltering yarrow.

WOOD THRUSH.

The silent world lies all asleep
    Beneath the silent moon,
Wood thrushes sunk in slumber deep
    Will wake to singing soon;
In crowfoot cups bright dewdrops lie
As glistening tears in pitying eye,
The ardent sun will kiss them dry
    Before the burning noon.

Now one by one the birds awake,
    At once begin to sing,
And now the day begins to break
    As crowfoot blooms in Spring;
Now field and wood with song are gay,
With songs to welcome in the day,
Now thrush low trills his simple lay,
    A wonderful sweet thing.

Now weary world would go to sleep,
    The sun has gone to bed,
Now shadows o'er the meadows creep,
    The crowfoot hangs her head;
Now buttercups and lilies fold
Against the moonbeams pale and cold
Those noonday hearts of burning gold,
    Their good - night wishes said.

Now one by one the stars above
    Are lighted clear and bright,
And Primrose burns her flame of love
    To shed a softer light;
Now sparrow's song forgets to ring,
Her head is tucked beneath her wing,
Now only thrush is left to sing
    The weary world's "Good - night."

ARETHUSAS.

Within the crystal of the streamlet flowing
 Through hot June meadows, answers flower to
  flower,
 Its low banks crowd they bringing Beauty's
  dower
As fond Narcissus to the fountain going.

There much elated, green and crimson showing,
 They drink dissolvéd pearls at morning hour
 In cups of ruby, — fatal noontide power
Of rising sun their simple faith not knowing.

Unhappy flowers, the first day of whose living
 Was last as well by Nature's plan intended!
 By seeking beauty your frail life was ended,
That fatal beauty, too, of your own giving!
Symbol of fate, — truth taught in fields and
 meadows,
Whose life is not defrauded by life's shadows !

SAND-PIPER.

In eastern light the ebbing tide
  Runs down the rippled shelving sand,
It leaves the beach uncovered wide,
  A smooth gray border to the land;
The low tones heightened by the tint
  Of rose reflected from the skies,
That silvered surface shows the print
  Of bird-tracks plain to peering eyes.

Thus stretching off in morning gray
  The long, pale line of watery beach
In curves of beauty winds away,
  Far as the challenged sight can reach:
But, lo! a presence comes between
  The rippling water's edge and me,
A bird's slight figure dimly seen
  En silhouette against the sea.

Not yet begins the meadow bird
  Its song of waking soft and clear;
Not yet is flute-like trilling heard
  From orchard tree, from thicket near;
But simple as the beauty found
  Between the ocean and the land,
At silent dawn is heard the sound
  Of plaintive piping from the sand.

FORGET-ME-NOT.

Forget-me-not, with eyes as blue
  As summer skies without a blot,
All wet with tears of morning dew,
Low-blending grasses looking through
  With wistful pleadings ne'er forgot;—
Dear flower, from year to year most true
  To look up from the self-same spot,
So does your lover watch for you,
                Forget-me-not!
  Forget-me-not! forefend the thought
That one who has of friends so few
  Should count your tender pleading nought!
  Ah, no! lamenting lonely lot
Of your abundandt grace I sue,
       "Forget-me-not!"

HUMMING BIRD.

A flash
As of a meteor bursting on the sight,
A sudden gleam of many - colored light
　　Shot from the burning heart of opal stone;
　　A dash
As of a falcon bold or swooping kite
Surprising quarry keen from its far height,
　　And all the vision instantly is gone!

　　A sound
Like that from quivering wings of honey bees
About the bursting bloom of orchard trees
　　An instant, now and then, is plainly heard;
　　A round
Of momentary visits such as these
Reveals as indistinctly as one sees
　　Bewildering flight of sun - bred Humming Bird.

MITCHELLA.

In midday twilight made by hemlocks old
That lean together in the somber woods,
Close grouped as kindred trees that fain would hold,
In whisperings low, communion here alone
Where seldom foot of curious man intrudes
To press the rounded stone
Plashed by the headlong rill
That tumbles down the hill,
And with green moss o'ergrown.
There creeps a beauty shy and low
Beneath the moss, beneath the snow,
For never does the green vine cease to grow
In summer's time of heat, in winter's time of cold.

Made glad with spring-time fancies pearly white,
Two tender blossoms on a single stem
In their sweet coral fruitage close unite
As rounded bead cut from a garnet red;
And all the year the vine, uplifting them,
Creeps on with cautious tread,
As if between soft palms
Its treasure safe from harms
Was borne above its head.
Proud of a beauty that abides
Through all the long year's changing tides
While in the wolf's-foot deep herself she
hides,
Mitchella shows her jewels with delight!

PE-WIT, PE-WEE.

Sing, little songster in the tree,
  From thy full heart out-pouring
The very soul of minstrelsy,
The joy the morning brings to thee
  As to the lark up-soaring;
Sing o'er again thy song for me,
Pe-wit, pe-wee — pe-wit, pe-wee,
And chant with gentle ecstasy
  The hymn of thy adoring.

Sing o'er and o'er again for me
  That song the stillness breaking;
Right well those simple notes agree
With thy life hid in a lilac tree,
  The noisy world forsaking:
Repeat once more, and then, please thee,
Pe-wit, pe-wee — pe-wit, pe-wee
The sweetest verse of all shall be
  'Mong the verses of my making.

SWEET-BRIAR.

In a basin 'mong the hills there lies,
Blue and clear—the image of the skies—
Water resting under noon-day bright,
Sweet resort of fancies gay and light;
  There among the flowers
  Birds are gaily singing,
  Happy, happy hours!

At the margin of the lake there grows,
Climbing to the air, a sweet-briar rose,
Forming with its vine, its leaf and flower,
O'er the blue, inverted heavens, a bower;
  Its perfume sweet is pleasant,
  By favor of the breezes,
  To lord and peasant.

From western hill-tops, when the day is done,
Falls on the rose the strange light of the sun,
Two opening buds make all the sweet-briar gay
These both appearing on the self-same day;
  With moisture teeming
  The chill air turns their breath
  To tear-drop's seeming.

When in the east again the morning shows,
On from the rising sun a bright ray flows,
It breaks upon the briar's buds young and tender,
Two lovely roses bloom in morning's splendor!
    Then the dew-drops pearly
    Perfume the air about
    In the morning early.

BOBOLINKS.

Always happy and gay,
   With a voice that's always in tune,
Swinging on willowy spray
In the meadows over the way,
    Swinging and singing with all their might
    In the summer morning's amethyst light,
      Sit the musical bobolinks;
   And out of their tuneful throats
   A song of magical notes,
   Liquid and melting, floats,
      Softly rises and sinks
   On the warm sweet breath of June.

Loud and louder they sing
   In the joy of life and of light,
Wider and wider they swing
Till they rise on fluttering wing,
    Straining and straining their throats to pour
    The joy from their full hearts brimming o'er
      In a shower of musical rain;
   And that flood of song, heaven - born
   With the golden light of morn,
   Shed over the dewy corn,
      Charms with the sweetest of pain
To an ecstasy of delight.

Falling and hovering low
  Over the young brood warm in the nest,
Lullaby cadences flow
Tenderly, vanishing slow;
    As at first the rollicking jollity rose
    Now soberly lapses the lay to its close
      In the sweetest accents of love.
  Lost are the birds to our view,
    Yet tremulous notes come through
    Bright sparkling crystals of dew
      Bending tall grasses above
Sweet hearts loved by bobolinks best.

NODDING THISTLE.

Adown the slope the breezes bring
    From hazels growing by the wall
Sweet tender lays the linnets sing,
    The robin's loud and anxious call;
But softest, sweetest note to-day,
    Heard on this quiet cattle-stead,
Bright goldfinch weaves into his lay
    While swinging on the thistle-head.

Adown the slope the breezes bring
    Soft breath of brambles budding new,
Faint odors sweet that fondly cling
    Round clover wet with early dew;
But sweeter than the breath of these,
    More potent than their rich perfume,
Is fragrance sweet that calls the bees
    Around the nectared thistle-bloom.

Adown the slope the breezes bring
    Dead needles loosened from the pines,
As butterflies on painted wing
    Go wandering where sweet summer shines;
But lighter than these needles dry
    Blown from the tall pine's swaying crown,
Upon these silent winds float by
    White silvery flocks of thistle-down.

KINGBIRD.

Harsh tyrant of the air,
With fear regarded, not with love,
Not charming with the sweetness of thy song
Nor with the beauty of thy plumage fair,
Thou dost compel obedience from the throng
Of birds that haunt the copse and grove,
By readiness to dare.

The careless passer-by,
The hawk intent upon his prey,
Swift sliding down the fields on easy wing
Upon the timid mouse has fixed his eye
And deems its capture is an easy thing,
Till in disgust he turns away
On hearing thy sharp cry.

Thou hast for ready aid
The swallow rushing into fight,
For such fierce bird unequal match alone,
But by example most courageous made;
His cause he thinks one common with thine own;
Right quickly puts the foe to flight;
Safe, being not afraid.

ST. JOHN'S WORT.

How cheery, warm and bright
With golden yellow light
The hillside pasture this midsummer day,
As through the fragrant fern
The starry flowers burn
With all the brilliancy of noontide ray!

Was it for this of old —
This blazing gleam of gold
From petals shining as from altar flame —
For token of their praise
That men in olden days
Should give St. John's Wort for this flower's name?

Because its flame was seen
Kindled in pastures green
At time when he, the Baptist, came on earth,
Of whom it was foretold
By sainted prophets old
That many should have gladness in his birth?

When came the year around,
With birch and fennel bound,
This flower our fathers hung above the door
In mother England dear,
And so they brought it here
To keep that home remembered on this shore.

YELLOW-THROATED WARBLER.

Fond lover of a lonely spot
    Deep in the silent wood
Where hound and huntsman enter not,
Where undisturbed by shout or shot
    The heron rears her brood,

To-day beside a meadow stream
    My stealthy steps intrude
Upon the water's quiet dream;—
Proclaimed by loud kingfisher's scream
    I break this solitude.

Here in lithe birches leaning o'er
The sleepy pool's low muddy shore
    This hot, still day in June,
I hear thy voice from clear throat pour
    A marvelous sweet tune,
Just spy thee on the birch twigs swinging,
Thou yellow-throated warbler singing;
      Lilting, tilting,
      Tilting, lilting,
That swaying movement timing
Thy music's bell-like chiming
    Rung pendulous and slow
Till Echo's startled clamoring is stilled
    To thy sweet singing low;
Till with its rhythmic melody the air about
    is filled,
And with responsive ecstasy thy listener is
    thrilled.

HAREBELLS.

Swinging, slowly swinging,
  Harebells rise and fall;
Clinging, closely clinging,
  To the mountain wall;
Swinging, slowly swinging,
  Harebells fall and rise;
Ringing, ever ringing,
  Music to the eyes.

Chiming, softly chiming,
  With the summer breeze,
All their music timing
  To the waving trees;
Ravished with the seeing
  Gladly would we know
For what favored being
  Tones of harebells flow.

Blesséd, happy creature
  Harebell tones that hears,
Mystic sounds of nature
  Silent to our ears!
Oh, ecstatic pleasure,   ·
  Theme for seraph's tongue,
Listening to the measure
  From the harebells rung!

VESPER SPARROW.

The summer evening, warm and still,
　Hears crickets chirping loud and clear;
From darkening woods below the hill
Hears veery's low, soft, liquid trill
Chime in with waters of the rill,
　'Neath alders, running near.

Sweet, too, the strains of music heard
　The dusty wayside hedge along,
Out-matching charm of chanted word
From heart of man, when heart of bird
With joy of life and love is stirred
　To sing her even-song.

'Tis from the bay-wing sparrow's breast
　Is poured this melting music free,
She sits above the secret nest
Where lie dear hearts she loves the best,
Sings all the chirping brood to rest
　With this low melody.

For weary toiler passing by
　This strain his heart with feeling stirs,
He hears the young ones' twittering cry,
Their mother's soothing lullaby,
Hears notes of rapture mounting high,
　Thanks God for cares like hers.

SWEET MARIGOLDS

Sweet marigolds, so fair and bright,
  At dawn so early waking
To watch the coming of the light
That streaks the east with pearly white,
  Above the hill-tops breaking;
All day ye follow with delight
The sun, and keep his face in sight,
Then weary close your eyes at night
  As if to ease their aching.

We see you turning towards the west
  To watch your regal lover;
The loyal feeling thus expressed,
The passion burning in your breast
  Is easy to discover;
But far from easy to be guessed
The dreams that in your quiet rest
Turn you once more to that fond quest
  Before the night is over.

KINGFISHER.

Companion meet of heron and of loon,
    Haunting with these the marge of sluggish stream,
Or sunken shore of overflowed lagoon,
    More lonely making this with savage scream;

Dead blasted tree blanched by rude wind and storm,
    Wrapped ghostly skeleton of withered birch,
Its white robe slipping from its shrunken form,
    Outstreches bare white arm, a proffered perch.

Here dost thou sit in the hot summer's day
    Silent and motionless, thy piercing sight
Close tracks the path of unsuspecting prey,
    Shy pickerel glancing in the noonday light.

That search unceasing is the watch still kept
    By Halcyon waiting on the island shore;
That patient heart and eye have never slept,
    They look for Ceyx coming nevermore.

That darting flight through bushes by the side
    Of sedgy marshes in the opening spring,
Recalls that morning when the maiden died
    And met her mate, restored on equal wing.

Men say thy back received its coat of blue
    From skies unclouded when the Flood was done,
Then caught thy breast its gorgeous tawny hue
    In that long flight towards the setting sun.

BOB WHITE.

What tender, plaintive call
    In notes of singing bird
    From the wood's edge is heard
In waning summer or in early fall,
    Repeated o'er and o'er so clear.
    We wonder, as the name we hear,
      Who is this lonesomo sprite
      That wants Bob White ?

When dawns the eastern day,
    When all the birds awake,
    Join in the song to make
Young morning's gladsome roundelay,
    We hear among the liquid notes
    From swelling hearts and straining
      throats,
      That pleading tone invite
      "Bob White! Bob White!"

When evening's level beams
    The longer shadows throw,
    And these the faster grow
Across the meadow s and the streams,
    We hear above the even-song
      That winsome calling clear and strong
        Chime with the last good-night,
        " Bob White! Bob White!"

Is it that 'mong the birds
    A myth goes with the phrase,
    As in these later days
Old faiths are veiled beneath our words ?
      As Hylas at the spring was sought,
      Eurydice from Hades brought,
        Is called some errant wight,
        " Bob White! Bob White!"

HARDHACK.

About half-buried boulders, overgrown
  With cold gray lichens and with patches round
  Of yellow moss set in concentric rings;
Upon rough surface of the weathered stone,
  There stubborn hardhack bold disputes the ground
  With creeping vine, and to its refuge clings.

Not fed upon by any browsing herd,
  Protection only claiming from the hoof,
  And having this from pasture rock and wall;
Retreat well noticed by sagacious bird
  Whose nest has hardhack leafage for its roof,
  And close rose-tinted racemes over all.

Among wild native bushes creeping fast
  O'er our neglected fields and pastures bare,
  How frequent is the blooming hardhack met!
Its fragrance breathing of a happier past
  When in the mother land with thoughtful care,
  A favored shrub, 'twas in the hedgerows set!

SPEEDING THE SWALLOW.

The summer's nigh! fly, swallow, fly!
  The welcome news conveying!
The burden of thy twittering cry,
The omen presaged to he eye
That marks thy flight across the sky,
  Admit of no gainsaying.
A homesick longing makes thee hie,
Thy anxious cares have urged thee by
  The summer winds delaying.

The winter's nigh! fly, swallow, fly,
  To overtake the summer!
For she hath left our northern sky,
Hath left her flowers to freeze and die;
Her friends without a last good-bye,
  As little doth become her.
Hasten thy flight; but here must I
Bide till the spring, in hope to spy
  Thee then the earliest comer.

CARDINAL-FLOWERS.

What royal standards these,
What banners in the breeze
That steals adown the brookside beneath the maple
    trees?

The stream is running low,
Its noisy waters go
Light rippling over worn stones under the August
    glow.

Both sides the stream to-day
Unfurl red flags and gay,
As if confronting armies here were drawn up in
    array.

What passion could intrude
To this lone solitude
To cause the banners of these hosts with blood to
    be imbued!

Or is it civic scene,
Brave escort of a queen,
Or function of the Church or State that in this dell
    is seen?

The cardinals to-day
Are coming up this way,
And with their deep-ensanguined cowls they make
    this brave display.

BLUE JAY.

October woods with light are all aglow,
  Their summer paths, dim as monastic aisles,
Are lighted now from golden leaves below,
  Through golden leaves above the sunshine smiles;
As flames the redbud in the early spring,
  In Indian summer bright the sumach burns,
Gay as gay butterflies on painted wings
  To red and gold the broad swamp maple turns.

Gnarled oaks take slowly on their russet brown,
  To twilight paleness silent beeches fade,
Long ash leaves in the morning flutter down,
  Their dark green deepened to a violet shade;
The noisy jay comes with its startling cry,
  'Mid yellow leaves of maple takes its perch;
A bit of blue in gold, as if the sky
  Were seen in patches through the faded birch.

GOLDEN - ROD.

When in its silvery husk the ripening maize
    Turns all its summer-treasured wealth to gold,
When up and down the field round pumpkins
      blaze, —
    Benignant planets on our vision rolled —
Within the corners of the gray stone wall
    Bright yellow golden-rod, of summer born,
Shows with the milkweeds and rough thistles tall,
    Itself just blooming when matures the corn.

It bears proud summer's banneret of gold,
    Full spread and flaunting, into early fall,
Defies the frost, defies September's cold,
    A hardy outcast, triumphs over all,
With gipsies tenting by the dusty way,
    Preferring spots unkept by human care,
Warms with its golden light the year's decay,
    And saves the deepening shadows from despair.

BLACKBIRDS.

The stillness of our late September days
  Is broken in upon by shrill-toned voices,
The call of crow, the saucy scream of jays,
  The scolding rant in which chipmunk rejoices;
Among them all the blackbird's frequent note
  Comes from the field-side wood, a constant
    chatter,
A loud complaining from so many a throat
  No mortal man can tell what is the matter.

The wheat and rye were garnered long ago,
  All birds are free to glean upon the stubble,
Blackbird and jay share with the crafty crow,
  How can it be that there is any trouble?
And yet the blackbirds drown the noisy jays
  By keeping up their everlasting clatter,
I wonder if one bird knows what he says,
  Or one that hears finds out what is the matter.

On mischief bent, the crow forbears to preach,
  The chipmunk's cheeks are much too full of barley,
Perchance the busy jay forgets to screech,
  On no occasion blackbirds fail to parley;
Discordant notes are showered from the tree
  As on the shingle roof the raindrops patter,
It is a blackbirds' gathering at high tea,
  And what the gossip means it does not matter.

FRINGED GENTIANS.

Late do you come, alone
Beneath our chill October skies,
To meadows stretching on beside the stream,
As if you had not known
The long procession which had gone before
Since when the crocus opened first its eyes,
First woke from its long dream
And, peeping through the snow, saw with
surprise
Pale daffodils once more;
Heard bluebirds blithely sing
'Mid Winter's sudden rout the coming of the
Spring.

You have not seen the bloom
Clothe leafless orchard trees in pink and
white,
You have not seen the oriole in his pride,
Seen golden-flowering broom
Run over rocky slopes as runs the flame
Of forest fires burning in the night
Along a mountain's side;
Nor have you come in time to catch a sight
Of our home swallows tame,
Who all the summer long
Skimmed over fields made glad with bobolink's
gay song.

Now field's are brown and bare,
Dull, sober, lying under sober skies,
And only now is chirp of cricket heard;
Along the wood's edge where
Of late the thrushes trilled a pensive song
The screaming jay across the open flies:
In color, flower and bird
As noonday cloud and shadow harmonize.
To neither do we wrong
By saying both are blue
To show that Nature's good - night thought is true

PURPLE FINCH.

Brown - coated bird that loves to sing
While poised upon a rapid wing,
Content in leafless woods to stay
Beneath November's skies of gray,
    How sweet to hear
    Those few notes clear
    Ring out on days else sad and drear!

Red - hooded cousin to the warm
Pine Grosbeak braving winter's storm,
Is it for him you patient wait
Round clumps of pine and spruce so late ?
    For him you sing
    The song you bring
    So early back again in spring ?

Or are you loth as we should be
To leave the cheery chick - a - dee,
Have you a longing in the spring,
As we, to hear the blue - bird sing ?
    Or do you find
    Among our kind
    Companions suited to your mind ?

ASTERS.

The hunter's moon, this cold October night,
    Sheds silver light,
On either side attendant, left and right,
    Stars sparkle bright.

Beneath that glittering splendor, hard and cold,
    Through æther rolled,
Along the border line 'twixt field and wold
    Pale stars unfold;

Late asters waiting till the waning year
    Shows foliage sere,
Till from the stubble cricket's chirping clear
    At night we hear.

These are the stars attendant on the nod
    Of golden-rod,
Thick as in spring-time dandelions trod
    The velvet sod.

With these, in clustered constellations found
    On fallow ground,
Shedding their starry radiance around,
    The year is crowned.

BROWN CREEPER.

Shy, silent dweller in the lonely wood,
    For fond mates having cheerful chick-a-dees
    These gloomy days of winter when the trees
Stand naked, shivering, as if dryads stood
Trembling for fear of footsteps that intrude
    With thought of havoc where will summer breeze
    Call with soft fragrant breath luxurious bees
To feast on nectar and ambrosial food;
For thy sweet sake let not this solitude
    Lose strength to shield, or charm it has to please,
The timid chicks of Nature's blameless brood.
    Here in these tops of hemlocks gray one sees
How thoughtful Nature, ever kind and good,
    Spreads tempest-proof, round sheltering tents for
        these.

WITCH-HAZEL BLOOM.

Oh! bitter cold the winds and strong they blow
  From northern hills across the frozen lakes;
They fiercely drive and mock the falling snow
  That fills the air with dizzy, whirling flakes.

The summer voices all are hushed and still,
  There is no hum of insects in the grass,
The frost forbids the babbling of the rill,
  Beneath the ice the waters silent pass.

On oak and beech still cling the russet leaves
  To frozen branches in this season drear,
Through those dead lips the shivering dryad grieves
  The vanished glories of the happier year.

From leaden skies flock out thick flakes of snow,
  On downy wings of frost they soft alight,
And on the brown-striped hazel twigs below
  With golden bloom show stars of silver white.

These yellow petals opening late and rare
  To grace the thicket when the year is done,
Seem, in their pearly setting, e'en more fair
  Than poppies blushing in the summer's sun.

CHICK-A-DEE.

Chick-a-dee,
Chick-a-dee-dee-dee-dee-dee,
This bleak December day
Sings the titmouse light and gay,
In his close and comely wrap,
In his black and jaunty cap,
While the air is full of snow,
And the icy flurries blow
  Bitter cold;
When the ice is on the stream,
And the sleeping chipmunks dream
  Dreams of old;
In the woodland all around
Wailing winds of winter sound,
Swaying branches snap and creak,
Pines and hemlocks groan and shriek.
Music sweet of singing bird,
Only blithe and gay is heard
  Chick-a-dee,
Chick-a-dee-dee-dee-dee-dee,

Chick - a - dee,
Chick - a - dee - dee - dee - dee - dee;
How that cheery, merry note,
Sounded from a happy throat,
All this nook among the hills
With a quickened memory thrills!
How its rich and sweet content,
To the gloom of winter lent,
Gladdens me!
Not the lonesomeness that's here,
Not the dying of the year
Saddens thee.
In the leafy woods of June
When the thrushes are in tune,
When the thickets are all gay
With the warbler and the jay,
Pipe for memory again
This same cheerful winter strain,
Chick - a - dee,
Chick - a - dee - dee - dee - dee - dee.

.

.

www.ingramcontent.com/pod-product-compliance
Lightning Source LLC
Chambersburg PA
CBHW020751020726
47495CB00008B/2374